Sweet as a SMURF

THE SMURFS 2

adapted by Natalie Shaw
illustrated by Dynamo Limited

Simon and Schuster
First published in Great Britain in 2013 by Simon & Schuster UK Ltd
1st Floor, 222 Gray's Inn Road, London WC1X 8HB
A CBS Company
Published in the USA in 2013 by Simon Spotlight, an imprint of Simon & Schuster
Children's Division, New York.
SMURFS TM & © Peyo 2013 – Licensed through Latig Belguim / I.M.P.S. The Smurfs 2,
the Movie © 2013 Sony Pictures Animation Inc. All Rights Reserved.
All rights reserved including the right of reproduction in whole or in part in any form.
A CIP catalogue record for this book is available from the British Library
ISBN 978-1-4711-1828-9
Printed and bound in the USA
10 9 8 7 6 5 4 3 2 1
Visit our websites:
www.simonandschuster.co.uk
www.smurfs.com

This is the story of Smurfette. The Smurfs think she is the smurfiest thing since sliced smurfcake—but sometimes she feels different from the other Smurfs. After all, she didn't start out as a true-blue Smurf . . .

You see, the evil wizard Gargamel created her and sent her to Smurf Village as his spy. The unsuspecting Smurfs found her in the forest and welcomed her back to their village. It was the smurfy thing to do.

But they soon discovered that Smurfette wasn't very smurfy at all. She was very naughty—so naughty that most of the Smurfs wanted her to leave soon after she came to the village. Everyone except Papa Smurf. He could see the good in her, even though she wasn't showing it.

With love, kindness, jokes, more love, delicious fruit pies, long walks—and a secret magical formula—Papa Smurf turned her into the sweet Smurfette we know and love today.

"The Smurf family is now one bigger," said Papa Smurf.

All of the Smurfs cheered . . . and fell in love with Smurfette on the spot.

But every year, on the night before her birthday, Smurfette had a bad dream. She dreamed that she wasn't a true-blue Smurf, and that she was really evil like Gargamel. When she woke up crying, Papa Smurf was by her bedside to comfort her.

"If I'm not a true Smurf and I don't want to be like Gargamel, who am I? Where do I belong?" she asked Papa.

"It doesn't matter where you came from, Smurfette," Papa Smurf said. "What matters is who you choose to be . . . and you are as smurfy as any Smurf can be."

This year, on the morning of Smurfette's birthday, no one wished her a happy Smurfday. She walked along the edge of Smurf Pond feeling sorry for herself. She didn't realize that the Smurfs were planning a big party for her and were trying to keep it a surprise.

"How could they forget my birthday?" Smurfette asked her reflection. "I guess I will never truly be a Smurf."

Suddenly a strange creature rose up through the water.
"Please! Help me! I escaped from Gargamel," said the small creature. "He created me."
"That means . . . you're just like me!" Smurfette exclaimed.
Smurfette was thrilled! She had never had a sister before.

But Smurfette's joy at finding her sister didn't last long. "I was just like you . . . before you turned good," said the creature, pushing Smurfette into the portal. "I've gotcha!" The Smurfs heard Smurfette yelling and arrived just as the portal closed. "She's been smurfnapped!" yelled Papa Smurf. "We have to save her!"

The portal took Smurfette to Gargamel's lair in Paris. It was all part of Gargamel's plan to get her to tell him the magic formula to create a pack of Smurfs, extract their essence, and use it to capture all the Smurfs.

"Welcome home, Smurfette," said Gargamel. "You've met your sister, Vexy. This is your brother, Hackus. Finally we're together at last. One big, happy family."

"The Smurfs will rescue me," Smurfette said angrily.

"Will they? After all, you're not a real Smurf," Gargamel said. "If you want to go back to them, give me the secret formula that Papa used to turn you into a Smurf."

Smurfette vowed that she would never betray the Smurfs. But as time passed, and it seemed the Smurfs weren't coming for her, Smurfette began to see that her new brother and sister weren't all bad. Smurfette remembered what Papa Smurf once said: "We rise to the amount of love we're shown, and we sink only when that love stops."

She taught Vexy and Hackus how to hug, and joined them on stork rides around Paris. She began to like Vexy and Hackus, and they began to like her too.

Meanwhile Gargamel pretended to be a kind, loving father. "Happy birthday, my dear,"
"You remembered my birthday?" Smurfette asked.
"Of course I did. We're family. I'm sorry your stepfather never came to rescue you.
Maybe this will cheer you up." Gargamel gave her a little figurine with a miniature
magic wand.

After a ride on the Ferris wheel to celebrate Smurfette's birthday, Gargamel took them to his secret lair, and the fun was over.

"Now, give me the formula," Gargamel said. "I'm your father. Give me the recipe for becoming a Smurf."

Smurfette still refused. But without the formula, Vexy and Hackus were fading away, so she gave it to Gargamel.

"I can't let them die," Smurfette said. "They're my family."

By now the Smurfs had found the lair and were waiting for the right moment to rescue Smurfette. They overheard Smurfette giving the formula to Gargamel and wondered if maybe she had turned bad.

Papa told them, "No matter what, she's family, and you never give up on family."

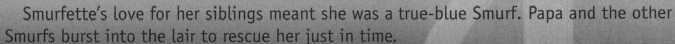

Smurfette's love for her siblings meant she was a true-blue Smurf. Papa and the other Smurfs burst into the lair to rescue her just in time.

"Smurfette!" cried Papa.

"You came for me?" asked Smurfette in disbelief.

"Of course we came for you!" replied Papa Smurf. "Was there ever any question?"

Smurfette was so happy to see her family again. And her new magic wand came in handy. She used it to get the Smurfs, and her new friends, the Naughties, back to Smurf Village!

When they returned to Smurf Village, the Smurfs surprised Smurfette with her birthday party. They sang the Smurfday song, ate blue velvet cake, and enjoyed being together. Smurfette's birthday wish had come true. She was home with her family.

HAPPY SMURFDAY!!

"Welcome home, Smurfette," Papa Smurf said. "You know, the formula for family requires just one ingredient: love."

And it was true. Smurfette loved both the Smurf family who raised her and the birth family she met in Paris. There was more than enough love to go around!